MAR 1997

PENGUIN PARADE

Robert J. Ollason

Lerner Publications Company
Minneapolis

NORTHPORT PUBLIC LIBRARY
NORTHPORT, NEW YORK

The publishers would like to thank the following people for their kind permission to reproduce photographs: pp. 6 (left), 9 (top), 10-11, 13, 14, 15, 17, Rick Price; pp. 6 (right), 7, 9, (bottom), 12, 18 (top and bottom), 21, 27, 29 (left and right), Annie Price; pp. 20, 22-23, 30-31, 33, Doug Allen; pp. 5, 24, 25 (bottom), 26, 34, 35, Edinburgh Zoo; p. 25 (top), Alan Thomson.

This edition first published in 1995 by Lerner Publications Company Minneapolis, Minnesota USA

Originally published in the United Kingdom in 1992 by Pan Macmillan Children's Books London, UK, in association with the Edinburgh Zoo

Text © 1992 by Robert J. Ollason
Illustrations © 1992 by Alan R. Thomson

All rights to this edition reserved by Lerner Publications Company. International copyright secured. No part of this book may be reproduced, stored in a retrieval system, or transmitted in any form or by any means, electronic or mechanical, including photocopying and recording, or by any information storage or retrieval system, without the prior written permission of Lerner Publications Company, except for the inclusion of brief quotations in an acknowledged review.

Manufactured in the United States of America

1 2 3 4 5 6 – I/JR – 00 99 98 97 96 95

CONTENTS

PENGUINS IN THE PAST

Imagine a penguin flying! We all know penguins can't fly. Usually we picture these seabirds waddling across the ice and snow in Antarctica, where many penguins live. Their wings look more like the flippers of a dolphin than the wings of a bird.

But long ago, between 70 and 100 million years ago, the ancestors of today's penguins could fly. Probably these ancient birds began to spend less time flying and more time diving under water to catch their food. They were seeking their **prey** at deeper levels than other seabirds. Their wings and feathers gradually **evolved,** or altered, to help them "fly" through water, rather than through air. Today, penguins are better swimmers and divers than any flying bird.

The oldest known fossils of penguins are about 50 million years old. They were found in the New Zealand area in the South Pacific. By examining fossil bones, experts have discovered that penguins in the past were about 5 feet tall. That's almost as tall as the average person. The tallest penguin living today, the emperor, is between 3 and 4 feet tall. Although very large, ancient penguins were probably much like present-day penguins in other ways.

Penguins Today

There are now 18 known **species**, or kinds, of penguins. They range in size from the big emperor of Antarctica, who can be 4 feet tall, to the little blue penguin of southern Australia, who is usually only 16 inches tall. The average life span of medium-sized penguins in the wild is between 10 and 15 years.

All species of penguins live in the south half of the world. But not all penguins live in icy Antarctica, as many people think. In fact, one species, called the Galápagos penguin, lives in the Galápagos Islands on the equator. The temperature there averages 88° Fahrenheit (though temperatures can often be much higher). Penguins are found mainly along the southernmost coasts of Africa, South

King penguin

Rockhopper penguin

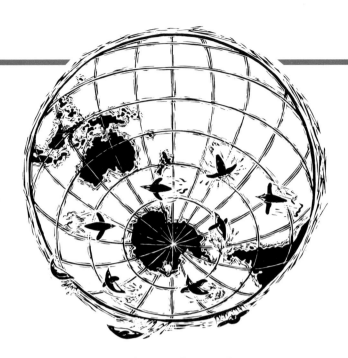

Above: Penguins live in the Southern Hemisphere, many of them in and around Antarctica and on the islands north of the continent.

America, and Australia. Many are found on islands in the Southern Ocean (the name some geographers use for the waters surrounding Antarctica). The only species of penguins that are true antarctic dwellers, breeding on Antarctica, are the emperors and Adélies.

All penguins have dark backs and white fronts. This coloring helps **camouflage** them. Seen from underneath in the water, a penguin's white front feathers blend with the light of the sky above the water. That protects the penguin from being spotted by **predators,** animals who hunt penguins. Seen from above, a penguin's dark back is hard to make out against the bluish gray of the sea below it. So the camouflage works two ways!

The colors of the beak and feet of penguins vary from species to species. All species of penguins also have either their own special patterns of feathers around their heads, or uniquely shaped bands on the upper part of their chests. These patterns are easy to see as a penguin swims on the surface of the water. They probably help penguins recognize members of their own species when at sea and when pairing off with a mate for

Below: *Magellanic penguin*

the first time. (Penguin partners recognize each other by their voices after that.)

Adélie, gentoo, and chinstrap penguins are elegantly patterned in black and white only. Magellanic, Humboldt (or Peruvian), Galápagos, and jackass (or black-footed) penguins sport bold black bands across their chests. The colors gold, lemon yellow, and orange feature strongly in the faces and chests of the kings and emperors. Crested penguins, such as rockhoppers and macaronis, have vivid gold and orange fans of feathers, or **crests**, above their eyes.

Penguins' feathers are short and lie close to their bodies, like fur, making the birds look smooth and sleek. The outer tufts of a penguin's feathers are oily, so the feathers are completely waterproof. At their base, the feathers are soft and downy. This layer of down traps air, which helps the birds stay warm in the coldest weather. As extra insulation, penguins also have layers of fat under their skin. Their feathers keep in about 80 percent of their body heat, while the fat keeps in most of the remaining 20 percent.

Macaroni   **Chinstrap**   **Magellanic**   **Emperor**   **Yellow-Eyed**   **Royal**
            with   **with**   **Jackass**
            chick   **chick**   **Little Blue**

Penguin Diets

The king (left) has a long, sharp, slightly curved beak, whereas the rockhopper's beak is shorter and not as sharp.

Penguins eat a variety of fish, such as pilchards, sardines, and anchovies. They also eat squid and tiny, shrimplike crustaceans called krill. Some species of penguins prefer one or the other of these foods, which keeps them from competing for the same prey. But many penguins can adapt to eating a wide range of prey, if necessary.

Scientists think that five million Adélie penguins eat 9,900 tons of krill and small fish every day. One gentoo's stomach was found to contain the remains of 960 krill. A young rockhopper being fed by its parents held the remains of 369 squid!

Penguins' beaks are designed for these different foods. Kings and emperors have long, sharp, slightly curved beaks designed to grasp large squid (some squid are more than 15 inches long). Rockhoppers eat smaller fish and have short beaks. Adélies rake their food to the back of their throats with their large tongues.

Penguins swallow their food whole. They maneuver fish to the back of their throats to make sure that the fish go down headfirst. If not, the fins could stick in the birds' throats, making it impossible for them to swallow. There are tiny spines on a penguin's tongue and inside its mouth. These spines keep fish and squid from slipping or wriggling out of a penguin's beak.

Once the food has been swallowed, it goes into the penguin's **crop**, a pouch in a penguin's throat where food is stored until it can be digested. A penguin can swallow only as much food as it can hold in its crop at any one time. But the crop is like a stretchy bag, so it can hold a lot. For example, an emperor can carry about 6.6 pounds of fish and squid in its crop.

DESIGNED TO SWIM

All penguins are similar in their general build. Their solid and smooth bodies are well **adapted** to their environment. Many penguins spend as much as half their lives at sea—more than any other seabird. So they have developed a streamlined shape. Penguins look a bit like torpedoes—pointed at both ends, particularly at the head—with no sharp angles to slow them down as they speed through the water.

As they have evolved over the centuries, penguins' wings have developed into stiff, bladelike flippers that push the

These chinstrap and Adélie penguins look like torpedoes.

birds through water. They are so powerful that they seem to fly just under the water's surface. A penguin's feet and tail, pointing backward together as the bird swims, act as rudders to help it steer.

We now know quite a lot about the time penguins spend on land, but we have learned much less about the long periods they spend at sea. We do know penguins are expert divers. Emperor penguins tagged with radio transmitters have been recorded diving to a depth of almost 900 feet. But most penguins find their food between 32 and 65 feet below the water's surface. A penguin can hold its breath for about 3 minutes while it is under water. Most humans can hold their breath for only about 1 minute. Emperor penguins have been known to stay below the surface for as long as 18 minutes, but this is rare.

Penguins are also strong swimmers. They swim very fast under water and can change direction with lightning speed. Most penguins can swim steadily at speeds between 4 and 6 miles per hour, but they can move faster in short spurts when necessary. Speeds of almost 9 miles per hour have been recorded, but some penguins may swim even faster.

Penguins have become such skilled swimmers and divers so they can catch their prey, who live at varying depths in the sea. Penguins often swim long dis-

Rockhopper penguins jump into the sea.

The leopard seal (above), *the killer whale* (top right), *and the shark* (bottom right) *eat penguins.*

tances searching for fish, squid, and other prey. The emperor has been found as far as 620 miles from land, but this is unusual. Some of the smaller penguins stay close to shore, not venturing more than 7 to 9 miles out to sea.

Penguins swim together in big groups for safety, trying to discourage predators such as leopard seals, fur seals, killer whales, and sharks. A leopard seal can skin a penguin in midair before swallowing it whole! The seal bites off a penguin's feet and flicks off its feathered skin by shaking the penguin vigorously.

Although penguins swim together in groups, they probably work alone to catch their food. Scientists rarely have seen penguins hunting together.

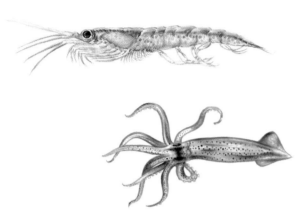

Penguins like to eat krill (top) and squid (bottom).

Like dolphins, penguins sometimes leap right out of the water to breathe without losing their speed, direction, or rhythm. This way of swimming is known as **porpoising.** Some scientists think porpoising helps confuse the penguins' predators. Others think it may be useful for keeping up speed over long distances.

One of the most amazing feats penguins perform is an acrobatic jump from the water to the shore. They shoot upward out of the water from a horizontal swimming position to land on either rocks or ice. First they eye the height of the ledge where they plan to land. Then they dive under the surface of the water and launch themselves forward into a leap of more than three times their own height! They manage to do this by swimming at speeds of over 6 miles per hour, then grasping with their toes as they land, using their flippers at the same time to keep their balance.

Porpoising penguins

LIFE ON LAND

Although they are well suited to life at sea, penguins, like all birds, need to spend some time on land. They have to be out of the water both to **breed** and to **molt,** or shed.

Penguins swim and porpoise through the water gracefully, but they are more awkward on land. Some people think penguins are funny-looking birds, perhaps because of their hunched shoulders and waddling walk. They look almost human as they shuffle along or huddle together against freezing winds. Although penguins look awkward to us as they walk or run, walking is natural to them. They get around well in other ways, too.

Many penguins travel long distances inland from the water's edge to nest. Emperors and Adélies often prefer to **toboggan** on their bellies over smooth snow and ice when they have a long way to go. Instead of walking, they speed along by kicking with their feet and pushing, or "rowing," with their flippers.

Other penguins, such as the smaller rockhoppers and macaronis, nest on cliffs

Adélies tobogganing across the ice

or other high, rocky surfaces. They have become experts at jumping up and down from rock to rock. Beating the air with their flippers to keep their balance and keeping both feet together, they jump higher and higher, gripping the rocks with their sharp, strong claws and beaks.

During the breeding season, penguins court, mate, and **incubate** their eggs. This

15

period may last two months or more. Most species of penguins gather in huge colonies, or **rookeries,** during this time. A million or more penguins may live in one colony. The yellow-eyed penguin is the only species that does not gather in groups.

When the breeding season is over, penguins molt their old feathers and grow new ones. Without the oily waterproofing of feathers, penguins cannot swim. So they must continue to stay on land during this time—about three or four weeks. Since they cannot hunt, they have to live off their store of fat.

The penguin's natural predators—seals, sharks, and whales—live in the sea. For this reason, penguins enter the water carefully. In some areas, such as New Zealand, humans have introduced animals such as ferrets and cats, predators who hunt penguins on land. A penguin is an easy target for these predators, since it doesn't naturally rush to the water for safety.

Penguins court, mate, incubate their eggs, raise their young, and molt on land.

Courtship and Breeding

The breeding season for penguins usually starts at the beginning of summer in the Southern Hemisphere, which is the beginning of winter in the Northern Hemisphere. The actual month in which breeding begins varies from species to species.

Many species return to the same colonies every year. Most males return to the colonies before the females. They claim their own territories by pointing their beaks toward the sky, calling loudly, and waving their flippers to and fro, in what is known as the **ecstatic display.** The ecstatic display attracts females and lets other males know the territory is occupied. An emperor's ecstatic call can be heard over half a mile away.

Many penguins seem to pair for life, or at least for a number of seasons. Penguins have elaborate courtship rituals and special patterns of behavior that they repeat at the start of every breeding season. Different species of penguins have slightly different courtship patterns. These patterns and rituals help strengthen the bond between a pair of penguins. For example, penguin partners often give each other pebbles, bowing and pointing their heads to the sky as they sing together.

A *chinstrap penguin holds a pebble in its beak.*

This ritual may reduce any fear or aggression between partners before they mate.

For mating to take place, the female lies on her stomach while the male climbs onto her back. Steadying himself by beating his flippers, he brings the opening under his tail into contact with the opening under hers. Then his sperm passes into her body so that the eggs will be fertilized when they are formed. Sometimes the partners also vibrate their beaks together while they are mating, or the male nibbles the feathers on the female's neck.

After mating, eggs form inside the female. Most penguins lay two eggs, but kings and emperors lay only one. Once eggs are laid, both the male and female of most species spend time incubating them. Incubating means keeping the eggs warm and constantly turned, to protect the developing chick inside.

All species of penguins except the emperors and kings lay their eggs in nests. Different species of penguins build different kinds of nests. Many make their nests in hollows on bare ground, with piles of stones, or in grass. Several species nest in burrows. Occasionally, penguins on Snares Island near New Zealand nest in the lowest branches of trees. In

Courting display by king penguins with a chick in the background

the Galápagos Islands, penguins nest in caves.

Male penguins usually incubate first, since the females have used up a lot of energy laying eggs and urgently need to feed. In the case of emperors, only the males incubate the eggs. Depending on the species, incubation can take between about 5 and 13 weeks.

A *pair of king penguins are courting.*

18

Rearing the Young

Most penguin chicks look quite different from their parents in color and pattern, ensuring that they are not mistaken for adults. If the chicks looked grown-up, they might be pecked and injured in the daily hustle and bustle of the colony. The first feathers chicks have are soft and downy, keeping the chicks warm. In some species of penguins, chicks molt their first set of feathers and grow a second coat of juvenile feathers. Last of all, their adult coat grows in.

The first set of feathers and the juvenile feathers are not fully waterproof, so chicks cannot go into the water. Although most baby penguins grow quickly, it can take a long time before they get their adult coats. Only then can young penguins swim and hunt and fend for themselves. For example, the gentoo chick first enters the water at 3 months of age, but the king penguin chick is 10 months old before it can swim and fend for itself.

In the meantime, a penguin chick is fed by its parents. The parents fish at sea and then return with food. They store the food in their crops until they return. When a penguin chick is hungry, it taps on one of its parent's beaks. The parent then regurgitates, or coughs up, the partly digested food.

Sometimes before a chick's meal reaches its beak, the food is snatched by a bird called the sheathbill. This white, scavenging bird looks much like a pigeon. It swoops toward an adult feeding a chick, knocking the chick sideways so the food splatters on the ground. The sheathbill

Emperor chicks molting

then grabs the meal and flies off to feed its own nestlings. Adélies have found a way around this problem: a chick puts its head right into its parent's throat to feed.

By the time they are several weeks old, penguin chicks need a lot of food. Often both parents must leave their chicks in order to hunt. In some penguin species, such as emperors and Adélies, the chicks huddle together in large gatherings called **crèches** while their parents are away. Sometimes there are several hundred chicks in a crèche.

Crèches are the perfect way for chicks to protect themselves from the bitter cold, especially in the Antarctic, where the temperature is often around −40° Fahrenheit. As the chicks huddle together, those on the outside of the group gradually move into the center, and those in the middle move outward. That way, every chick has its share of warmth from all the bodies pressed together.

The crèches offer safety from predators too. One of the chicks' chief predators is the brown skua, a large, gull-like scavenger. Skuas dive-bomb nesting sites, stealing both eggs and stray chicks. But

A gentoo mother feeds her two-week-old chick.

neither skuas nor another enemy, the giant petrel, will attack a tightly packed crèche.

Even when chicks are with a parent, they aren't completely safe from predators. Often skuas work in pairs. One distracts a penguin parent while the other seizes an egg or a chick. Instead of at-

A *king chick* gets fed by its parent.

tacking the center of a colony, skuas concentrate on the nests on the edge, where it is easier to separate a chick from its parent.

Penguin parents returning from the hunt with food for their chicks have to find their chicks first. The penguin species with nests and territories can find their chicks easily. Other species, who leave their young in crèches, have to find their own babies among all the others—and they all seem to look exactly the same! Parents recognize their chicks by the sound of their voices. In a big group of birds, it can take some time for parents to find their families. The adults always wander and search until they are sure they have found their own chick. They never feed the wrong one.

Usually, both penguin parents are closely involved with incubating their eggs and rearing their young. Even with such good care, it is common for penguin chicks to die because of the harsh conditions in which they live. Sometimes the parents' only chick is lost. When there are a pair of chicks, often only one of them will survive.

EMPEROR PENGUINS

The world's largest living penguin is the emperor, who can grow to almost 4 feet tall. The emperor and the Adélie are the only two species that breed on the continent of Antarctica. And the emperor and the king are the only species to lay a single egg and build no nest.

Of all the penguins, the emperor lives farthest south. Its breeding habits show how well it has adapted to the very cold climate in which it lives and rears its young.

Emperors breed in June—as winter begins in the Southern Hemisphere. The emperor male takes the precious, newly laid egg onto his feet, and covers it with his special flap of belly skin. He incubates the egg in this way for about 60 days, during the long, dark winter. The temperatures can drop as low as −70° Fahrenheit.

Often the males eat almost nothing during the courtship season. They continue to go without food during the two months after courtship when they incubate the eggs. During this time of fasting, they may lose half their body weight! Only birds the size of the emperor could lose so much weight and still survive.

Male emperors huddle tightly together in crèches, as their young will do later, while they incubate their eggs. They can walk while balancing their eggs on their feet. So those on the outside of the group gradually move toward the center of the crèche, making sure that no bird spends too long in the bitter cold on the outer edge. Because their bodies are pressed so closely together, the emperors lose far less heat than a single bird would if he stood alone.

Few other species of birds could gather in large groups of males without fighting or pecking. But emperors have had to

Male emperors are incubating their eggs.

adapt to their cold environment. They have become less aggressive so that they can benefit from each other's warmth during the long incubation period.

Emperor nesting colonies are often far from the sea, sometimes nearly 60 miles. While the emperor males incubate the eggs in the colony, the females trek the long distance back to the sea. They feed and fatten themselves so that they will be ready to take over the parenting duties when their chicks hatch.

As soon as the chicks are ready to hatch, the fattened females return, ready to feed their babies. If a chick hatches

before its mother returns, the father feeds the newborn chick a milky liquid from his crop. This liquid can keep a chick alive until its mother returns from the sea.

Once the females take over caring for the chicks, the males can at last set off to feed. Later on, the edges of the sea ice melt, bringing the open sea closer to the nesting sites. Then both parents can go back and forth to the ocean to gather food for their fast-growing young. The emperor chicks call to their parents and bob their heads up and down when their parents return. The chicks' bold black, white, and gray pattern probably makes it easier for the adults to spot them in the semidarkness of the Antarctic during this season.

By the time the short antarctic summer begins in October or November, the chicks are ready to strike out on their own. They gather together on **ice floes,** sheets of ice that break away from the edge of sea ice. The floes float northward into the warmer waters of the Southern Ocean around Antarctica. During the journey, the chicks molt and grow their adult feathers. Then they can finally enter the sea and catch their own food.

KING PENGUINS

Kings are the second largest of the penguins, growing to about 3 feet. They raise their young on the islands north of Antarctica, never breeding on Antarctica itself.

Like the emperor, the king penguin lays a single egg and has no nest, incubating the egg on its feet instead. But unlike the emperor, the king penguin does have a territory. And instead of just the male incubating the egg, as emperors do, both the male and female king penguins incubate their egg. They take turns, gently rolling the egg between them to transfer it.

The king is the only penguin—and, in fact, the only seabird—who doesn't breed every year. Kings breed twice in every three years because their chicks are too large and slow-growing to be hatched and reared within a single season.

There may be several thousand pairs of king penguins in a nesting colony, plus young chicks at different stages of development. The colonies are busy places, with nonstop bustle and activity.

King penguin eggs take 54 days to

The king penguin incubates its egg by nestling it under a special fold of skin.

hatch. After their first covering of grayish down, king penguin chicks develop a thick, soft coat of brown feathers that does not molt until the chicks are 10 months old. Until then, their feathers are not waterproof, so they cannot swim or go into the water at all.

Gentoo Penguins

Gentoos are about 2.5 feet tall. Triangles of white feathers grow between their eyes and meet on top of their heads. Their beaks are a bright orange-red, and their feet are fleshy pink. There are two types of gentoos: the northern and the southern. The northern gentoo is usually slightly bigger than the southern.

Like king penguins, gentoos live among the islands in the Southern Ocean around Antarctica. Gentoos seem to be one of the least aggressive species of penguins. Sometimes southern gentoos create mixed colonies with chinstrap and Adélie penguins.

Gentoos often nest on raised beaches and sometimes on hillsides covered with clumps of tussock grass. They make their nests using pebbles and bits of moss. Some of the older, more experienced birds lay their eggs on clumps of dead grass to make sure that the chicks are kept dry when the frozen ground thaws in the warming weather.

Above: A *gentoo parent with six-week-old chicks*

Below: A *gentoo resting in the sun*

Gentoos often nest on raised beaches, but at zoos they use nesting rings.

Gentoos are one of the few penguin species to change their nesting sites from year to year. This may be because small ticks breed among the moss from which gentoos build their nests, and the ticks may irritate the birds. Gentoos usually lay their eggs in November, as summer begins in the Southern Hemisphere, much later than emperors lay eggs. Gentoo chicks become independent when they are about three months old.

ROCKHOPPER AND MACARONI PENGUINS

Rockhoppers are common on many of the islands north of Antarctica. They measure about 2 feet tall. Their golden yellow crests look like long, bushy, upward-sweeping eyebrows. Their eyes are red, their beaks are reddish brown, and their feet are pink. Of all 18 penguin species, rockhoppers are perhaps the most aggressive toward people and toward each other.

Rockhoppers are good swimmers in rough water, and they probably spend the whole winter at sea. When on land, they have a unique way of getting around. While other penguins tend to waddle when they walk on land, rockhoppers jump or bounce with both feet together. Straining their heads forward, they balance themselves by pointing their flippers backward. In the breeding season, they hop up high cliffs and steep slopes covered with scree (small rocks that pile up at the bottom of rock faces). Clinging to smooth rocks with their strong, sharp

Rockhoppers use a well-worn path to climb up to their colony.

27

Rockhopper with chick

claws and beaks, they look for nesting sites above the sea. Rockhoppers make their nests on ledges, in crevices, and sometimes in the shelter of huge boulders. When the chicks have hatched, the parent birds hop up and down the cliffs many times a day to fish, returning with full crops to feed the hungry babies.

Above: *Rockhoppers wait in line to hop off of a cliff.*

Macaroni penguins are closely related to the rockhoppers. The two species look similar; in fact, macaronis are often mistaken for rockhoppers. The crests of the two species are slightly different, however. While the rockhoppers' crest plumes are yellow, the macaronis' crests are more orange than yellow. And the macaronis' crests grow from a kind of center parting on top of their heads, rather than from just above their eyes. This unique crest gave the macaronis their name—it looks a little like a hairstyle once popular with young Englishmen. Some of these young men formed a club in 1772 called the London Macaroni Club and called themselves the Macaronis.

Other Penguins

long with the emperors, the Adélies are one of the penguin species scientists study most often. There are probably more Adélies than any other type of penguin; there can be over a million birds in a single colony. Adélies are among the noisiest and most aggressive penguins, perhaps because of the huge populations of their colonies and their need to defend their territories.

Jet black backs and heads make Adélies easily recognizable. Adélies also have distinctive white circles around their eyes. The black feathering comes farther down their beaks than in most species. Adélies are a little over 2 feet tall.

Like the emperors, Adélies breed as far south as Antarctica, but they sometimes nest farther north alongside chinstraps and southern gentoos.

Chinstraps got their name from the thin black line that runs under their chins. It resembles the chinstrap of a black hat or helmet and makes them look like little soldiers. Chinstraps are similar in size and weight to Adélies. Both chinstraps and Adélies are closely related to the gentoos.

Several species of penguins live in parts of the world that are too warm for a penguin's comfort. The jackass penguin comes from South Africa, the Humboldt penguin from South America, and the Galápagos penguin from the Galápagos Islands.

These penguin species do swim and feed in cold ocean currents, however. Jackass penguins swim in the Benguela Current off the southwest coast of Africa. Galápagos penguins can be found in the Cromwell Current near the Galápagos Islands, and Humboldt penguins travel

in the Humboldt Current off the eastern coast of South America.

These penguins have all adapted to cope with the heat when they are on land. For example, they nest in burrows or holes where they are protected from the sun. They can lose heat through bare, featherless patches on their faces. And they can also lose heat through their flippers, which are larger in proportion to their bodies than those of other penguins. The face patches and flippers give out heat like radiators!

The little blue, or fairy, penguins live in New Zealand and Australia. They nest in burrows, but more for protection from their predators than from the heat. They do not make the lengthy ocean excursions of some other species. In fact, they rarely go to sea for more than a week at a time.

The little blue penguins are the only penguins who are **nocturnal,** or active at night. They come ashore in the dark to feed their young. Near the city of Melbourne in Australia, their nighttime arrival from the sea has become a tourist attraction. They strut up the beaches and climb up steep slopes to their burrows, without seeming to notice the excited tourists at all.

The yellow-eyed penguins of New Zealand nest in cool forests. They do not breed in large colonies as most other penguins do. Instead, their nests are often scattered over a wide area.

The yellow-eyed penguin is one of the rarest species, along with the Galápagos penguin. Only about five thousand pairs of each species can be found in the world.

Adélie penguins

Penguins in Captivity

Penguins have been a great attraction in zoos for many years, and most of the world's major zoological collections have a penguin exhibit. In the past, most zoos were in countries with a warm climate. The Humboldt and the jackass thrived better than other penguins in captivity, because they are from places with a warm climate too.

Emperors, Adélies, and chinstraps often suffered from heat exhaustion if they were kept in zoos. They could not cope with the heat of European and American summers. But recently, new technology has made it possible to keep these species comfortable even in warmer climates.

Zoos have also become more successful at breeding the animals in their col-lections. More and more zoo animals are giving birth to healthy babies, so fewer animals are being caught in the wild. Some of these animals are endangered, so not only are zoos being less of a threat to wild populations, but they are increasing numbers of certain species.

Penguins have not been easy to breed in captivity, although some zoos have been successful with certain species. Scientists are trying to find ways to improve this. Zoos share information about breeding successes and failures, which helps speed up progress.

Sea World in San Diego, California, probably has the most high-tech penguin exhibit in the world. It cost seven million dollars to build! Huge and air-conditioned, it is home to Adélie, rockhopper, and emperor penguins. The exhibit's saltwater pools and air are carefully filtered to prevent the spread of disease. Visitors can stand on a moving walkway and watch through glass as the birds move about and swim in their antarctic-style setting. Sea World achieved a "first" when an emperor chick was successfully hatched and reared in 1980.

A few zoos in different parts of the world have also built expensive, modern

Penguin enclosure at Edinburgh Zoo

King penguins in the wild form colonies. The first king penguin chick to hatch outside the Antarctic was bred at the Edinburgh Zoo in Scotland in 1919.

exhibits. The Milwaukee Zoo in the United States and the Ueno Zoo in Tokyo, Japan, are examples. All are doing a great deal of scientific research to try to improve the breeding of penguins in captivity throughout the world.

The first king penguin chick to be hatched and reared outside the Antarctic was bred at the Edinburgh Zoo in Scotland in 1919. Since then, many kings have been successfully reared at Edinburgh, together with dozens of gentoo chicks, for which the zoo is world famous. The gentoo penguins in most of the world's zoos today were originally supplied by the Edinburgh Zoo.

The Edinburgh Zoo began exhibiting penguins in 1914. It was supplied with wild birds from the Antarctic by a whaling company until 1963. After 1963, the penguin colonies at the Edinburgh Zoo—especially the gentoo colonies—have been self-sustaining.

Penguins will always be popular with people. Visitors love to watch the Edinburgh Zoo's daily penguin parade in spring and summer. Hundreds of people line the route as the penguins march out of their enclosure and around the area just outside. The birds do this freely, without seeming to mind the excited crowd of people watching them.

PENGUINS AND PEOPLE

The first penguins known to Europeans were the jackass and magellanic species. They were discovered during the voyages of Vasco da Gama in 1497 and Ferdinand Magellan in 1519. Other species did not become known in Europe until the eighteenth century. In other parts of the world, however, penguins were known long before this time by the native peoples who lived near them.

Penguins are great favorites with people of all ages. Perhaps they remind us of ourselves, with their upright stance, their careful walk, and their black-and-white patterns, which can look like a tuxedo or a waiter's uniform. In zoos they are always popular and entertaining.

But people have not always treated penguins well. In the last century, whalers hunted penguins by the thousands. The whalers, who also hunted whales and elephant seals, boiled down the carcasses of these animals to extract the oil from their blubber. Whaling was a thriving industry, and it took a heavy toll on penguin populations.

Humans have also killed and eaten penguins and penguin eggs in the past. Some early sailors might not have survived without penguin meat. Hunting penguins for food probably did not hurt penguin populations overall. But the gathering of eggs was a serious problem. For example, over half a million eggs of jackass penguins were once gathered

each year in South Africa. In some places, gathering penguin eggs is now illegal.

Today, people are affecting penguins mainly in two ways. First, people are competing with penguins for food. For example, the slaughter of many of the great whales, who eat krill, has left much more for penguins to eat. For that reason, certain species of penguins have increased in numbers. But people are now beginning to catch and use krill for food, so the penguins who benefited from the extra food may begin to suffer.

Fishing fleets off the west coast of South America and around the coasts of South Africa also compete with penguins for food. They fish for anchovies and pilchards, which are prey for Humboldt and jackass penguins. Such fishing could threaten the penguins' food supplies.

The second way in which people threaten certain penguins is through oil spills from tankers. Two major sailing routes for tankers are around the Cape of Good Hope at the south tip of Africa and through the Strait of Magel-

lan at the bottom of South America. Oil from the tankers is often spilled when the tanks are cleaned out. The resulting oil slicks can injure or even kill the jackass and magellanic penguins who swim in these areas.

In some areas, humans have introduced predators such as ferrets or cats that hunt penguins on land. Over the years, yellow-eyed penguins in New Zealand have suffered badly from such predators, who were not originally their enemies. People have also cut down many trees in the forested areas where yellow-eyed penguins nest.

Being aware of such problems can help us find solutions. Penguins are unique creatures, survivors in some of the harshest habitats on earth. We must make sure that they have the protection they need to survive.

Penguin Facts

When they are on land,
penguins sometimes rest by
leaning back on their heels and supporting
themselves with their stout, stiff tails.

Most penguins do
not live more than 10 years,
though emperors may live as long as
20 years.

A penguin's flipper
cannot be folded like other
birds' wings. Its wrist and elbow joints are
fused, and the only movement is at the shoulder.

The emperor is the
only penguin that never sets
foot on true land. When it is not in the
ocean, it lives on the frozen sea ice around Antarctica.

Emperor penguins
are much less likely than other
species to pair for life, possibly because
they have no nesting territory to go back to. Studies
have shown that 78 percent of Adélie partners form
lifelong bonds, while only 14.5 percent of emperor
partners mate for life.

An emperor has 75
feathers on every square inch
of skin.

Breeding emperor
penguins have to put up with
the coldest conditions of any bird, with an
average temperature in the Antarctic of −40 Fahrenheit.

Adélie breeding
colonies have been known to
contain more than a million pairs of birds.

GLOSSARY

adapted–physical changes that occurred to a group of animals that makes survival easier

breed–to produce young

camouflage–to blend into one's surroundings

crèche–young penguins that stay together for warmth while their parents are away. Male emperor penguins also stay in a crèche while caring for their eggs.

crests–showy tufts of feathers on a penguin's head

crop–a pouch in a bird's throat where food is stored before it is digested

ecstatic display–the dance ritual penguins perform during courtship

evolved–changed over time

ice floes–large floating sheets of ice

incubate–to keep eggs at the right temperatures for chicks to develop and hatch

molt–to lose an old set of feathers before a new set grows in

nocturnal–being active at night

porpoising–swimming by leaping out of the water, without losing speed

predators–animals who hunt and eat other animals

prey–animals who are hunted and eaten by other animals

rookeries–places where large numbers of birds lay their eggs and raise their young

species–a group of animals or plants that share special characteristics

toboggan–a way penguins travel on smooth snow or ice. They slide on their bellies, kicking their feet and flapping their flippers.

Metric Conversion Chart			
WHEN YOU KNOW:	SUBTRACT:	then MULTIPLY BY:	TO FIND:
tons		.91	metric tons
pounds		.45	kilograms
miles		1.61	kilometers
feet		.30	meters
inches		2.54	centimeters
(degrees) Fahrenheit	32	.56	Celsius

INDEX

J598.4   Ollason, Robert J.   \14
OLL
          Penguin parade

$19.95

DATE			

MAR 1997

NORTHPORT-EAST NORTHPORT
PUBLIC LIBRARY
151 Laurel Avenue
Northport, NY 11768

BAKER & TAYLOR